Froilan's, Ltd.

A Collection of Poems

Froilan "Puroy" Manalo

Ukiyoto Publishing

All global publishing rights are held by

Ukiyoto Publishing

Published in 2023

Content Copyright © Froilan "Puroy" Manalo
ISBN 9789360499259

All rights reserved.
No part of this publication may be reproduced, transmitted, or stored in a retrieval system, in any form by any means, electronic, mechanical, photocopying, recording or otherwise, without the prior permission of the publisher.

The moral rights of the author have been asserted.

This is a work of fiction. Names, characters, businesses, places, events, locales, and incidents are either the products of the author's imagination or used in a fictitious manner. Any resemblance to actual persons, living or dead, or actual events is purely coincidental.

This book is sold subject to the condition that it shall not by way of trade or otherwise, be lent, resold, hired out or otherwise circulated, without the publisher's prior consent, in any form of binding or cover other than that in which it is published.

www.ukiyoto.com

I dedicate this book to my professor, Ma'am Neneth Ramiro-Rondera, and to my nephews Paul and Jiroh.

Acknowledgements

This book can never be complete without the help of my dearest friends.

Special thanks to my professor, Ma'am Neneth Ramiro-Rondera, and to Sir Chris Opeña Orcuse, for all the advice and support in accomplishing this gargantuan task. I also thank my boss, Sir Alex Occidental for convincing me to have my works published. Many thanks goes to Ma'am Dianna Bodoso and to all those who reacted to my FB posts, for inspiring me to keep on writing. Also worthy of mention, thanks to the Pisonet internet café that let me use their desktop PCs.

This collection of my works wouldn't have been complete without your support. Thank you all.

Soli Deo Gloria.

Contents

Introduction	1
Behind The Glass	2
Spilled Days	3
Principles	4
Have Mercy On Me	5
Convert To Cash	6
Prosaic Existence	7
The Resemblance	8
The Flower	9
To Whom It May Concern	10
Memento Mori	11
Double Sonnet	12
Ars Poetica	14
Extinction	15
Sonneto Uno Y Media	18
The Last Horse	20
Heir Loss	21
Yellowed Diploma	22
My Barrio By The Foothills	23
Sola Fide	24
Beyond Susanna Heights	25
Conceited Youth	26
Rogádo Ná	27

Tabula Rasa	28
Suffrage	29
The Unfinished Work	30
Let The Readers Tell	31
The Bachelor	32
Ang Cattleya… Bow!	33
My Fair Share	34
Sudden Death	35
Before The Autumn Leaves	37
Surrealism	38
Deceptive Sheen	39
Tides And Waves	40
The Healthy Books	41
The Poor Poet's Plume	42
The Purpose Of Reunions	43
Δόξα Τω Θεώ (Soli Deo Gloria)	44
The Reformed Bohemian	46
Sonnet Thirty-Seven: Personal Vendetta	47
The Show Is Over	48
The Prophecy	49
Wingless Time Flies By	50
The Donor	51
To John and Samuel	52
¿Donde esta, de Anda?	53
Winter Is A Grasping Hand	54
To the Women I Meet on The Pavements	55

My Orphaned Seedlings	56
My Old Typewriter	57
The Batch of Supermen	58
The Roses in The Bamboo Forest	59
The Lonely Invitation Card	61
My Manifesto	62
The Last Thousand Words	63
Τετέλεσται (Consummatum est)	64
For Mama	65
Nouveau Riche	67
The Nostalgic Prophet	69
The Promise	71
About the Author	*72*

Introduction

Poetry is a vital component of man's intellectual and spiritual wellbeing. It is the nutcracker that opens the shell for us to enjoy the edible and nutritious kernel.

In an age of social media, rhymed and metered verse must be promoted (along with other forms of poetry) for the benefit of our later generations. And this is my contribution.

Read it well, dear readers, and reread it if needed, and enjoy journey with me.

Behind The Glass

With just a narrow strip of light upon
Your windowpane, I see a dream shines through--
A slit through which I peek into a Heaven gone,
And felt a fever like a love so true.

I felt a thirst for you, an urge to see,
To sip your beauty in a vulnerable mug;
To taste the bittersweet fate that fell on me,
To drown in a sea of nectar like a drowsy bug.

The curtains covered my paradise view
And never will I ever partake of your face;
The one-way lover's road I never knew
Shall take me to a slowly ebbing grace.

I rather not possess your soul and mind
Than have you cold and so unkind.

Spilled Days

O where, I wonder where my youth has gone--
My strength, my youthful days, my hopes and dreams;
As if an ancient supernova shone--
It bursts but now without a single beam.
Excitement's gone-- for what should I presume?
All thing's the same, I've done it all before,
Again I'll do it in the morning (I assume)--
My tedious existence's such a bore..
Now grudgingly I walk (I used to run)--
If I could only have eight feet and arms,
A pair of phoenix wings to get things done--
To speed and strength please add some youthful charms.
If only zealous youth afresh can stay,
I'll spend it frugally another day.

Principles

There was a hallway, painted glossy black.
Most people walk there, never looking back.
With its façade aglow in crimson red,
Within its bowels we were blindly led.
But down the hallway was a golden door,
Behind was luxuries abound in store.

I could have followed what the masses do,
To where they go, I could have been there too.
I did not go where others blindly go,
My conscience against the traffic flow.
So out I went to the façade and saw
That we are willing slaves of our own laws.

I'd rather lie on a cheap, dewy bed
Than live and die on someone else's bread.

Have Mercy On Me

My Dear, have pity, my kind might end with me,
Please save my species now-- gone will it be.
I cannot procreate alone-- a bride
I need-- so hurry now before I'm dried.
  Make haste while we're still lustily fresh,
  While we may still use our borrowed flesh.

I may not live as long as we desire,
Before I leave this world, to you I must sire.
The tide of passion may ebb someday,
So take me now and let us do it someway.
  This life and chance why should we waste?--
  Our time is fleeting as a mare in haste.

My hope is in your hands-- to no one else--
So hurry, let us sound the wedding bells.

Convert To Cash

I care not what the future'll think of me,
To fill my hungry stomach, each poem a fee.
Today is what I care for, tomorrow's yours--
I have to live today and then our course.
  The classic fame you'll give me when I'm dead
  Will never be as good as keeping me fed.

Though some may build me monuments tomorrow,
It will not ease my pain and sorrow.
So pay the Piper while I'm apipin' now--
I have to feed my mortal body somehow.
  Posthumous medals, busts, an honoured tomb
  Will do me no good when I meet my Doom.

Why save my poems for posterity?--
I have to eat before I meet Eternity.

Prosaic Existence

Alone I sit, alone I stand and run--
Alone I weep, alone I reap the fun..
Alone I eat, alone I suffer hunger--
Alone I love, alone I broil in anger..
  I simmer in the heat, alone I'm cold--
  Alone I've worked, alone will I grow old..

Alone I triumph, alone I despair--
Alone I break, alone I repair..
Alone I save, alone I recklessly spend--
Alone I grow, alone will I meet the end..
  The nights are dark and long, but I am all alone--
  And the days are hued in melancholic tones..

Alone, alone, such a tiresome word--
Thesaurus, give me one more, for I'm getting bored.

Froilan's, Ltd.

The Resemblance

My son, forgive me if you're still unborn--
Your future mom has left my heart forlorn;
There's still a chance that she may do
Her part-- the other half of you--
  I cannot form you all alone,
  I need a sheath, a partner for my bone.

If she'll oblige, then lucky you, my child,
You'll get a chance to live, whether tamed or wild;
A doctor or a priest I wish you'll be:
From my sickness you will set me free.
  She is the key to your existence
  But I need some prayers against her resistance.

To form my likeness, another clump of clay
Is all we need-- so you may see the light of day.

The Flower

The orchids bloom hanging on a bough,
Iridescently pleasant-- transitory though;
"Such a beauty is beyond your reach,"
My simple peers did adamantly preach.
  So, underneath that bough I just admire
  And listen to the background music of a lyre.

'Though other blossoms may have better scents,
They cannot cause my heart some deeper dents;
The sweet perfume a rose may richly give,
Can't give my dying heart the will to live.
  Cattleya blossoms amidst the verdant trees,
  My eyes your velvety crimson beauty did please--

All other flowers wilt in mind,
But in my heart, your name is what you'll find.

To Whom It May Concern

Dear Sir or Madam, I, Puroy, a poet, male,
Of legal age, do hereby wish to mail
My literary works for you to print
So at this moment I may paint
  The contents of my pocket-- I'll give you a hint--
  Upon discovery I'm sure that you might faint.

I need the money-- Yes, I'm not a hypocrite--
My pen is like the Labyrinth of Crete--
So better pay my sonnets or I'll send it to
Some other printer who will surely do;
  It's worth the gamble, let the readers tell
  By counting all the copies we may sell.

Sincerely yours, the hopeful writer,
Who hereby beg for a future brighter.

Memento Mori

Why worry 'bout my getting old?
I may not live that long to feel the cold;
I might as well just live in peace alone
Than fear the coming of a time unknown--
  Our time will come as soon or as remote,
  Our present state of mind can ne'er denote.

Fear not what you will eat the coming years
Maybe tonight's your last, by morn we'll shed our tears;
Die young and pretty or die old and weary,
Whether bright and sunny or blurred and teary:
  The end's the same-- we all must sleep
  Unto the cold and dark repose and slumber deep.

Prepare thy self, the end is coming soon
And growing old is not a privilege nor boon.

Double Sonnet

The cold and lonely nights are fast approaching--
My knees are doomed to hurt with past reproaching;
Since my thirties I felt octogenarian--
Oh how I wish I'd been a vegetarian!
I've laboured in vain to feed this mortal flesh
With another creatures' flesh and grains others threshed.
  Inadvertently I've worn myself to die
  A slow and tiresome toil as capitalists lie.

I could have been a really rich man now
But now I felt I'll be as a butchered cow.
I've written songs for you to read and sing--
But entertaining you was not a small thing.
  My Dear Friend Readers, buy and read my book
  It would not hurt your pockets if you take a look.

I'll spend the money for another print
So you may read on and get a better hint

Of how it feels to be an early-aging slave;
And so that you may have me from debt be saved.
Poetry is art as painting's an art--
More pleasant to the senses than a fart.
  A book is a window into an author's life--
  You'll come to know him as you know your wife.

You'll get to learn from my past regrets--
A good advice you'll read and ne'er forget.
No marketing pitch is better than the book--
The quality of contents itself's the hook.
  I'll feed your hearts and feed your mind:
  You'll get to be wiser still while you unwind.

Ars Poetica

A Mac, a typewriter, Perkins, pen and pad:
I care not what is good for you or bad;
Just write, create a verse or eight,
Before it's apocalyptically late.
  Express your thoughts, your joy, your misery--
  And crack the shell of misty mystery.

Go out, see God's creation, leap and sniff the air,
Let nature moisten you-- with dew upon your hair.
Observe the sights and sounds and write them down,
Imagine some as green and some as brown.
  A poet paints the azure sky with words
  To pierce your lover's bosom like a dozen swords.

No Manifesto can vividly recount
A poet's thought-- and from oblivion surmount.

Extinction

As I was walking through a frozen world,
I came upon a forest white with snow.
No verdant needles, leaves nor buds exposed--
All white against the black of a moonless night.
The humankind was all but lost save me,
But I kept wandering in the hope to see
A fellow hominid with whom I may
Perpetuate my race before my day.
I trod upon the valleys and frozen lakes,
Through streams of ice and waist-deep mounds of flakes.
I know not how to start a cooking fire
So I ate raw venison caught in the wire
Of an abandoned cabin in the woods--
'Cause as of now I live on raw and faulty food.
No herb nor fruit on the ground can be seen
Just frozen carcass, raw and lean.
I wonder where the caribous went to graze
(By now my mind is in a static haze).
That dead dog chained by that abandoned house--

Froilan's, Ltd.

Shall be my supper, the side's a mouse.
By now you might be thinking that all was still--
But no! bears prowl and wolves howl upon a hill.
I'd better wait for them to starve and die,
And then I'll eat their cadavers where they lie.
The whole year round there are no geese nor ducks,
The candlelit house might have cheese, just given luck.
The door was locked within, I have to break in,
Broke a pane, there within, I flashed an evil grin,
For by the stove I saw victuals galore
And roasted turkey on the table by the door!
I ate to my heart's (tummy's) content until..
I heard a clatter on the floor-- then I stood still.
And slowly I approached the darkened porch
If only there's a handy torch).
An impish silhouette fled to the woods,
I ran after it but the snow did me no good.
So with much effort I did hopelessly chased
But so much exertion's such a waste,
For I lost the simian figure in the dark--
Just like an arrow that missed its mark.
I chanced to stumble upon a rotten log

And pulled an axe out from the heavy fog.
With such a bladed weapon now at hand,
I'm now the master of this barren land.
I searched for the apelike being-- where oh where?
It might be there, nigh here or yonder there.
The dawn was breaking when an antlered deer
Ran past behind-- I wish I have a spear.
Then suddenly out of the snow a hand tightly
Gripped my ankle in a flash of morbid fear--
With my axe I hacked its head not so lightly.
I heard the cracking of the skull out of the snow
(As yet what creature it was I do not know).
The hand released my ankle, motionless it fell.
When I saw what it was I let out a yell,
With much remorse I looked upon a woman's face--
I have just killed the hope of the human race..

Sonneto Uno Y Media

I wonder where you are, my love, my dear,
I've earned enough for us, so do not fear--
For now I have the means to feed a village,
Even if barbarians resort to pillage.
  My seven years beyond your age
  Just made me such a wiser sage.

I'm not a miser, just a little wiser
Than an unscrupulous rice merchandiser.
Experience taught me frugality,
Of costs of love and its legality.
  Nota bene life's brevity, beware,
  A lonely life may hurt you beyond repair.
Audacity beyond capacity
But that's the plain and simple verity.

All wealth can be attained, if God is willing,
But time can not be saved nor be regained--
Worry not about a married life's billing--

Just never let our hearts remain detained.
  A blissful life with you can be so thrilling,
  Like a paradise regained, its glory attained--
  'Though it kept on spilling, in love we remained.

The Last Horse

In the race of life, the swiftest wins,
We keep on running whilst the world still spins.
Our gifts and skills, our horses, talents, tools--
Should not be wasted with some indolent fools.
To win, you must go faster than the rest,
Outrun them all and give your bestial best.
  It is not over 'til you reach the line,
  If I get there first, then the cup is mine.

You chose a brief but glorious life,
But I will cross the line when the time is ripe.
For even if the world should gallop fast,
I will still leisurely trot 'til my days are past.
  Rush on, don't be outpaced, just reach the end,
  I might as well relax along the bend.

Heir Loss

My child, be you a daughter or a son,
Be you existent, or hopes be gone or none,
I leave you all my hard-earned hard-rock mansion
And all the implements for its expansion.
I care not if you'll be so ugly or so pretty,
As long as you'll be frugal, wise and witty.
  I lived a back-breaking life full of labour,
  So never spend it as a fleeting vapour.

My child, don't spend it on trivial vanities,
Consider my life-- without frivolities.
I've suffered weary hours and superhuman pains,
So thriftly use my gold on prudent gains.
  Be born, my child, wait for a timely mother,
  As for now, I'm yet your future father.

Yellowed Diploma

An empty pocket and a stub of pen,
An empty stomach and a college ring,
Some brazen medals but forgotten when
They came or what they meant or glories bring.
  I basked in praise-- O what a glorious thing--
  An envy of those voices in the dark,
  I am whom artists paint-- the minstrels sing--
  The public face that makes their fancies spark.

E'en though my hand have left immortal marks--
In paper, stone or in the minds of men--
I still perambulate these lonely parks
Like Roman ruins, now, an empty den.
  If beauty fades and glory flees awing,
  Then why did not gold and pleasures cling?

My Barrio By The Foothills

Malicboy forest, mountains, falls and tranquil streams--
Your rocks and mighty trees are still in my dreams.
I dream of days returning to your shade--
Such memories of you shall never fade.
Down your narrow valley was my childhood home,
Beneath heaven's dome, upon a fertile loam.
I wish we've never parted down the road--
The grief of leaving you is such a heavy load.
For half my life was spent on foreign soil,
And endlessly I suffered sweating toil.
But now I wish to return to you
And hope your welcoming heart is burning too.
If I were rich, by now I have a farm
And living off my latter years within your arms.

Sola Fide

O what a poor and piteous soul that's me--
Alas, my share is but a flaming sea!
I've been a sinner since I was conceived
And did the deeds before they were perceived.
O God, please save me from the ultimate grave,
I cannot save my soul-- myself I cannot save.
I'm just a man-- a not enough excuse--
But only You have the right to choose.
Please save me from the lake of fire--
My soul from hell, my body from the mire.
O Holy Father, only You can give
Eternal, holy, blissful life to live.
I'll live this present life for You, O Lord,
But give Your servant the will to follow Your Word.

Beyond Susanna Heights

My life had been a noisy rush of cars:
Forever running here and there or near or far.
I've lived a life of promptly chasing time--
Before I lose the might to furnish rhymes.
All haste, full gallop, fast as a gust of breeze,
My mind and hands must write before they freeze.
I rather be a hermit reading poetry,
Resting under an arátiles tree.
With coconut and bamboo groves behind me,
In front are golden fields of rice-- there you'll find me.
Secluded rest, repose, I love the silence,
But life's necessities have forced its sentence.
If only simple country life's enough for me,
Then city jobs I'll leave and I'll feel free.

Conceited Youth

Don't be so proud, for you're untrained and young;
Control, restrain your inexperienced tongue.
I've been there too, a quarter of a century--
You still not know 'bout luxury and penury;
Of youthful blooming and of fading beauty;
Of rising early and of neglecting duty;
Of teenage stamina and wilting strength;
Pity, you still don't have deep wisdom's height and length.
My hair is sadly gray, and you are gay,
Your dewy dawn against my darkening day,
But I stand firm, respected for what I say,
And from the truthful way, I'll steadfastly stay.
The mirror lies and tells you what you want to see,
So do not brag, for you are just a flea.

Rogádo Ná

My túgang, your sole hermáno, if magadán
Soltéro and máyô agóm, your son
Shall be my wealthy heir-- it's only fair--
If you survive me, you can have a share.
I've patiently buntál abacá and lukád,
And hid some gold in Milaór, and glad
That I'll be leaving fortunes for your child,
But never let yourself be beguiled...
...All wealth may come and go, and you may never know,
What Pol may do to what I sow,
He may not be as wise as what we've been--
Our sorrows he have never seen.
So teach him Prudence's proper way
So he may never from that day be led astray.

Tabula Rasa

What should I write? Absurd original,
Or works rephrased and be a criminal?
Should I write senseless, incoherent verse,
Or should I copy classics and be cursed?
Should art be pursed or art should burst?
And I'll rework the best, or write the worst?
How blessèd are the early generations--
They said the best and worthy of veneration.
It's hard to face a blank and empty page,
As words escape my mind-- like an empty cage.
But I should write in a different point of view,
So younger folks may learn things fresh and new.
A wordless paper is a dreaded thing
Yet I shall go on writing songs for you to sing.

Suffrage

I'm sorry, Sir, I can't accept that bill,
I firmly stand for the people's will.
Democracy was paid in blood and blasted flesh,
So in my heart, their legacy's still fresh.
Some gladly sell their privilege to choose,
And dignity immorally they loose.
I rather die impoverished with head up high
Than have my freedom flee and say goodbye!
So give your twenty dollars to someone else
Whose liberty he willingly sells.
A thousand pesos shall not suffice
To trade our heroes' priceless sacrifice.
Our children's future's in the ballot box,
Let Freedom enter where she calls and knocks.

The Unfinished Work

Forgive me if this verse was rendered incomplete:
Against my past achievements I can not compete.
I gave my best but lost imagery and rhymes
And rhythms as soft as melodious chimes,
Or craft poignant subtleties, soft and sweet
As how the nightingales and larks do sing and tweet.
I can not think of words to write
As bright and brilliant as the Northern Lights.
So finish what I've started where I failed
And publish it in print and have it brailled.
For I have plans for art and reading skills
To kill naïveté and other ills.
Fill in the blanks when I am gone,
Don't let my works be left undone.
Complete my works, for I...

Let The Readers Tell

I strive for quality but also more,
For the juicy pulp and its bitter core.
We eat the flesh and plant the inedible seeds,
We use the parts according to our needs.
Some sonnets sound harmonious to our ears,
Some madrigals can break our eyes to tears.
  The cacophony can be thrilling as the best,
  Or worse than an arrow to your chest.

I'll write the poems of lush and verdant fields,
Of sights and sounds my mind and pen may yield.
Just choose the best and tear the rest—
Assuredly some of it may pass the test.
  Some writings can destroy while others build,
  This pen can be a sword or else a shield.

The Bachelor

On being single at forty-one point five,
I'm glad that I'm independently alive.
My walking cane can wait a decade more,
And spectacles a quarter of a score.
I still can stand and walk, 'though I can't run,
But I must cause my Cause before the setting sun.
  My dusk has come but I've been worldly wise—
  I've scattered seeds before Time's gripping vise.

So treat me not as an untutored fool,
I've woven blankets, jackets made of wool
Ere winter comes, whilst chrysanthemums bloom,
I've been prepared before the nights of gloom.
  As Karen said, "We've only just begun,"
  I say: I'm just beginning to have some fun.

Ang Cattleya... Bow!

Cattleya summer— with soft and gentle breeze—
Your warmth I yearn against the winter freeze.
Your vibrant blooms against the green, green woods
Has caused glad, joyful, fragrant, vibrant moods.
Sakura bloomed too early in the spring
But summer's orchids are the tropics' king.
  Cattleya lovely blossoms, you're my Queen—
  No fairer flower I have ever seen.

'Though *sampaguita* spread her lovely scent,
Cattleya's still my cherished heaven sent.
For who can tell the smell of hell?
But I can tell her beauty all so well.
  Don't be deceived by their contrived cosmetics,
  For I esteem pure nature's virgin ethics.

My Fair Share

The penniless, poor penitent me,
Deprived of public pity as you see,
Unwholesomely bare naked in the street,
As passers-by invisible me they treat.
I beg for bread, no butter, just a bit,
To keep my miserable life and wit.
  All faded, ruined glory, relic of the past,
  Dim memories of wealth that did not last.

My life was spent on hoarding worldly wealth,
Unwittingly neglecting sound holistic health.
The orphans, widows, and those sick of heart—
I should have done a better start.
  From richest rugs to tattered rags,
  From crystal palace crib to rain-soaked crags,
  All faded, ruined glory, relic of the past,
  Dim memories of wealth that did not last.

Sudden Death

I wish I'll leave this life without me knowing,
As freezing breezes kept on blowing,
My soul to Abraham I'll go and rest,
I'll lay my head upon his downy breast.

"For life is but a fleeting moment,"
Your post is just a tweeting comment.
  In Paradise I pray we'll someday meet,
  And you the first of all I wish to greet!

(Your likes and hearts and stars and caring shares
Are not as good as sharing cares.)
I'm not afraid to meet my Sole Creator,
But I'll be glad to be your terminator.

(Your likes and hearts and stars and caring shares
Are not as good as sharing cares.)

"For life is but a fleeting moment,"
Your post is just a tweeting comment.

Your wife and children may not see
Your bones beneath the raging sea.
  In Paradise I pray we'll someday meet,
  And you the first of all I wish to greet!

Before The Autumn Leaves

O winter widows, spring will surely bloom,
And solstice sorrows shall be swept by summer's broom.
Your children are still young, and you are young,
You still can stand, the air is in your lungs.
Your husband has lived his appointed years,
He's born in tears, and yet he died in tears.
  You're younger, stronger than your older half,
  You still can walk and work with half a calf.

You have been born with your father's name,
But being married to this man, you share his fame.
And if he died too early, he is not to blame,
So never give his name a cause for shame.
  O winter widows, spring will surely bloom,
  Your children are still young, and you are young,
  All solstice sorrows shall be swept by summer's broom.

Surrealism

Four dozen tongues, my poems were published, boy!
That is way better than a monarch's joy!
I write in English but my heart's a native,
And thank my teachers that I've been creative.
I thank my publishers for giving laurel crowns—
I'm now the king of bums and clowns.
  I thank my critics for the positive reviews,
  My weeks are filled with media interviews.

Next tomes shall be for Pulitzers, Nobels,
And next to those, as poet laureate… Oh well…
Such dreams will drag the drier days,
Much cream will crack the criers' case.
  If these make sense, consult a psycho,
  It may have been the writer's typo.

Deceptive Sheen

I may not live as rich as mostly do,
But they may die disgusting as a poo!
This decrepit man, dilapidated shell—
At least I never shared a man-made hell.
I have outgrown my usefulness,
The fullness of which was spent on foolishness.
  Another shoe, another waistline to don—
  I'll doff the old and use some other con.

The ancients said what's new to them—
We'll have to cut their rough-hewn gem.
I'll start a modern trend that you must try,
But let me see its fruits before I die.
  I'll leave to where the poor do mostly go,
  But let my sonnets shine a glorious glow.

Tides And Waves

My end was spent beyond my meager means,
The fruit of thriftly eating grubs and greens.
I rise and fall just like the rhythmic tides,
But I never lay long immobile by the sides.
I always climb the hill towards the moon,
But fall beyond the other side so soon.
  My endless cycle of troughs and crest,
  May end by writing life's brief, brutish best.

We get rewards by ease or brutal work,
But we shall part by the highway's fork.
We'll leave the things our callous hands have made,
But they'll surely forget, as memories fade.
  Our endless cycle of troughs and crest,
  Shall end when we did find eternal rest.

The Healthy Books

Eight thousand portraits launched eight million ships—

A book, indeed, can cut the world into strips.

Some books may guide, like the Bible by the Prophets;

Some books bring harm, like Marx's— some fools cashed profits.

So always check the label, read nutritious books,

You'll never know the good and bad the author cooks.

  The truth you'll find if you just read

  The author's mind said by their words and deeds.

What you fill the pot is what you'll eat—

If you fill it with only wine, you'll get no meat.

A healthy soul is better than some healthy bones,

A healthy mind can reach celestial zones.

  So feed your soul with spiritual food,

  For it is Man's predestined good.

The Poor Poet's Plume

My Latin pen can penetrate all innocence,
You're *ignoramus* if it didn't make any sense.
My pen is sharper than a firmer sword,
But does not kill, but pleases someone bored.
My pen is longer, firmer than my nephew's quarter-inch,
And this, my pen, can stand the firmest pinch.
  But don't be green— my pen is tinted blue—
  It leaves an indelible hue for general use.

My pen can make this world a little sharper,
Among the apes you'd be a little smarter.
But still my pen should find a partner pad,
A paper proof to leave a harper sad.
  Preserve my writings, not my pensive pen,
  The proof is better than the tool of men.

The Purpose Of Reunions

It's nice to be with friends but better still to be
With uncles, cousins, aunts— all glad to be with me.
My nephews grew taller than their uncle dear,
Their children will grow taller in a year.
I hope we'll do it every June or spring—
The cold won't stop my knees from dancing waltz and swing.
  I'll *bailè* with my nieces, nephews, small as I,
  When the winds are warm and the ground is dry.

Most families meet when there's a wake,
But we should better dance around my wedding cake.
I pray we're all alive on my wedding day,
You're all invited to the venue by the bay.
  Be patient folks, I will get married soon,
  Just wait a decade more, you'll meet my bride some June.

Δόξα Τω Θεώ (Soli Deo Gloria)

To God be the glory, to my pocket be the money,

To Him, I'm sorry, but I should eat the honey.

My tithes shall go to Him while I'm alive,

And when I'm dead, the rest should go to His elected hive.

The residue is due to friends and kin,

I'll share to them my toughest ML skin.

  Just let me spend my hard-earned gold and fortune,

  I'll leave you all your best deserved choice portion.

Remember though, that He should have the fattest part,

And you must pick what overflows my cart.

He deserves the best for He's the fount of all that's good—

You must be satisfied your plate and table's filled with food.

  Don't touch what's His, for you shall have your share,

From Him came everything, so it is only fair.
So don't you worry, you would not be sorry,
But always keep in mind, to God be the glory.

The Reformed Bohemian

My lawn needs trimming as my chin needs shaving,
Such sloppy life should be worth saving.
My laundry lies neglected like a python's molt—
Such state ungroomed deserves a lightning bolt.
A Labrador to feed, it badly needed washing;
At least I had some fun with red lights flashing.
  The Friday gigs and willing, groovy chicks,
  Should compliment the itchy fleas and ticks.

The fun, fun, fun— funny that it never stops,
Considering my blood's potassium drops.
A lifestyle such as this should better end,
Than be a number in a statistical trend.
  Prolonged we suffer pain and pray
  That dandy Death should not delay,
  But better still to stoically stay
  Alive to settle the accounts to pay.

Sonnet Thirty-Seven: Personal Vendetta

I have already done a lot of deeds
To meet my fellows' human needs.
The things I've started are mostly complete,
And always I with Time compete.
I wish to live as long as people needs me,
I would not want some other hands to feed me.
  I hope to I'll live just long enough to see
  My works in print, the public reading poetry.

I'll reap the fruition of my hard-earned labour,
To live that long depends upon God's favour.
My books' proceeds should go to Godly charities,
And should not go to useless disparities.
  It's God at work, it is not what my hands have made,
  To Him the glory as my memory shall fade.

The Show Is Over

I've made you happy then, but now none other left
To satisfy old humour's stealthy theft.
I'll leave while the longing is hot—
Enjoy my memory left in the pot.
Those foolish rhymes we shared, those senseless ditties,
We've spent our lives just sitting on the jetties.
  The show is over, clap, the curtains drop,
  Remember there are days when laughters stop.

Chaplin's gone, and Dolphy's gone…
  And so must I…
Remember there's a day that I must die.
I want to exit this in fashion,
And line my casket with a cushion.
  So cry, don't laugh, this poem is not so funny,
  As morbid as it seems, my life had been sunny.

The Prophecy

Relax, your book will be complete, get published,
You'll live to know your legacy's established.
You will get married soon, have responsible sons,
And leave them bars of gold in metric tonnes.
You shall live and leave as poor as a mouse,
And give your children a gold and marble house.
  Relax, your life is at ease on a coffee mug,
  So take your time as slowly as a slug.

You've lived your life in loathsome labour,
And ate your spoil with much untasty flavor.
But eat you must the unsavoury food,
For you shall leave your sons the ultimate good.
  So keep on eating herbs and salted fish,
  Your sons shall have their every whim and wish.

Wingless Time Flies By

A pleasant sight it is, the early bloomers,
The children now have bloomed too soon, unlike us boomers.
We are the trekkies, sons are Jedis on foot,
Your grandchild can fly in an iron suit.
We used to play with marbles, rubber bands and cards,
These children play with Leila in my neighbour's yard.
  The by-gone years of nuclear fears,
  Are better than today's uncertain tears.

My child, don't be so proud your rank is mythic,
Before you were born, I was a mystic.
We're happier with what we had back then,
We're satisfied to have our notes and pen.
  Technologies may change and trends may change,
  Within necessities range, we're not that strange.

The Donor

I give my blood to save a life or two,
A time may come that I shall give my spare parts too.
These parts that I no longer need when dead,
Should benefit my fellow on a hospital bed.
Reduce, reuse, recycle all I'll leave behind,
We should not waste for such a heart you'll rarely find.
  A wooden heart, a heart of stone or gold,
  But rest assured, my heart is flesh and never cold.

My perforated lungs, my broken heart,
My fatty liver and some bruised parts—
Use all the functional entrails that you may need,
And let the junk the worms may voraciously feed.
  I to my Maker go, my fleshless soul,
  The cadaver shall descend to the six-foot hole.

To John and Samuel

Some lives are worth imitating, their deeds,
Their arts should not be left overgrown with weeds.
The lichens, mosses, the patina of Time,
Should be removed, raise art from oblivion's slime.
An artist sacrifices health, for art's sake,
And even spends his worldly wealth, for art's sake.
  John stood tiptoe upon a little hill,
  Keats brought us joy until he's very ill.

Their brief lives left us immortality,
Study we, regardless of morality.
In Xanadu did Kubla Khan decree
That Coleridge gets his Doctorate's Degree.
  Their lives were spent as transitory flowers,
  But spent concisely with enduring powers.

¿Donde esta, de Anda?

I thought there was a statue in the middle
Of this crossroad— an enigmatic riddle.
He used to be my landmark to the port,
But now he's gone— the theft did none report.
For half a decade I was living south and east,
I thought the markers should remain, at least.
  Simón, Simón, O where's the lighthouse by the bay?
  To the pier where my sweetheart did wait and lay.

Across the river, I can not recall,
Which corner should I turn to see the wall.
I felt by now her ship has already gone,
I'd better book a trip to her island home.
  Simón, Simón, have you eloped with my *Inday*?
  Return my darling joy, or else I'll die.

Winter Is A Grasping Hand

My brittle bones— they make me suffer much—
I felt that clay is stronger than my bones as such.
The cold is like the devil's fingers grabbing bones—
The cracking sound it makes is like sweet crispy cones.
The crunchy noise, the howling pain it brings,
The bravest boys shall run in rain and leave all things.
  The senior's discount is no good for me,
  I rather flee to where from pain I'm free.

Prolong not suffering and ease the pain,
So I can leave behind this cumbersome cane.
I rather live as young as sprinters on the beach,
Than live just sitting while my sitter feeds me peach.
  So horrible! these nights have been so Arctic cold,
  It better be my last than grow arthritic old.

To the Women I Meet on The Pavements

Why do you kept on giggling, laughing at my face?
Upon my mirror I can see no funny trace.
Whenever I pass by, your friends would shriek and stare,
As if I am endangered species deemed as rare.
I am a human being, heart's with feeling,
Insulted even though you find me thrilling.
  Imply not with insinuations, vague desires,
  Don't act as if you've touched a live electric wire.

Don't bare your teeth on me, O girls please listen,
'Cause when I smile, you'll know the stars do glisten.
I'm off to work so just don't bother me,
And when I walk on by, just let me be.
  So brace your hips and shoulders, keep from shaking,
  Resist the urge to faint, and no noise-making.

My Orphaned Seedlings

Don't cut down the tree too early in spring,
Wait for the summer fruits the blooms shall bring;
Or cut the scions, graft them on a younger stock,
Whose roots are unshakable as a rock.
The parent trunk is now beyond its age,
Be burned as charcoal, its life's final stage.
  Before you fell the tree, let it be fruitful,
  If not, as fuel it shall be more truthful.

Wait for the saplings, seeds and fruits— new cycle starts—
Then do what pleases you, and fill your heart.
Let the old tree wilt as useful as when still alive,
But the chance to procreate, to him you shouldn't deprive.
  Dried to the roots, the old tree shall die and fall,
  Nurture its young trees while they are soft and small.

My Old Typewriter

My battered *makinílya*, lying on a shelf,
Long rusty, dusty— as my self.
I used to oil it on my college days,
But now some ages passed since we parted ways.
We both grew old, its creaking joints and keys—
No better than my cracking feet and knees.
  Unused and unmaintained, inanimate or not,
  The grimy junkyard is our final spot.

The younger generations have replaced
The old school's antiquated ways and face.
We're phased out off the people's homes and stores,
We are no longer part of the progressive course.
  "Well done, my faithful servant," thus dismissed,
  At least we'll share a common shelf, ungreased.

The Batch of Supermen

We have been born too late, the latter decades
Of that century borne, as light on deck fades.
We are the last to feel the slippers hit our butts,
The last to sprinkle salt on burns and cuts.
Our elders have already died but taught us well
To walk and prosper over where they fell.
  We are the golden generation, sons of Clark,
  We are the heroes of our siblings in the dark.

We are the bridge of ages, then and now,
We'll teach them all we've learnt, the whens and hows;
As how our parents taught us wheres and whys,
We'll teach our children how to be more truly wise.
  We are the golden generation, sons of Kent,
  We are modern tribunes Nietzsche have sent.

The Roses in The Bamboo Forest

O listen to the sound that bamboo makes,
Its creaking nodes are drums on windy lakes;
The breezes whistles through sounds like a flute,
Its melodies are sweeter than the lute's.
The scent of innocence, so pure and virgin,
The winds brought to the groves, where delights converge in.
  So this is paradise, a garden in a grove,
  Its simple, naked nature, truer than a dove.

The place was lovely, tranquil for my soul,
But circumstances pull me to another goal.
The city lights are brighter, more colourful,
The rushing city keeps our coffers full.
They pay me well for suffering the urban noise,
I'll someday spend it when I'm weak to raise my voice.
  So this is hell, a golden mine with smoggy air,
  The city for my cherished grove— it's so unfair.

Froilan's, Ltd.

The Lonely Invitation Card

I made a card, a wedding invitation,
Upon my peers' indecent vindication.
I used my laptop, powerpoint at hand,
I cropped my pic as if I'm in a foreign land.
I stood half sideways on a dewy morn,
Amid a garden as the day was newly born.
  I typed as follows: "Froilan and (*blank*) nuptial day
  You're cordially invited on *My* wedding by the bay."

I think it's funny, making cards as these,
While there's no bride, just buzzing of the bees.
But there I stand, tuxedoed, hugging air,
And to the camera I smile and stare.
  Prepared was everything, except the bride,
  Still I proceed with prenup pics— none by my side.

My Manifesto

This is no new movement, revolution,
It's just a constant motion, evolution.
The poets' thoughts had old been said before,
That nothing's new, the hole shan't be rebored.
No manifesto's redder than tomato,
Nor content denser than a big potato.
  What makes a poem vegetably vibrant,
  Matters not as its difference with a hydrant.

Be it surreal or Romantic, classic,
The poet's craft should be as breezy plastic.
A poem is a poem and leave it as it is,
There is no better reason than what's in this.
  It's not incomprehensible, just sensible,
  That more like blood, the poem should be indelible.

The Last Thousand Words

There are some weary milestones in my files,
Of precious gemstones, though, in various cuts and styles.
I've been through seven pillars in four full moons,
I salted my potatoes in tablespoons.
Adventurous, this journey caused much painful piss,
My medications I usually miss.
  This travelogue should give me something good,
  For mankind's good, forget I sometimes eat my food.

This book of mine is yet one-eighths short 'til done,
The sleepless last mile won't be as fun.
The darkness comes but eastward tired I go,
The previous miles had been so painfully slow.
  My bones and flesh won't let me leap and run,
  Delay the setting of the golden sun.

Τετέλεσται (Consummatum est)

It's done! I'll rest assured my work is done,
I'm ready to face the setting sun.
The orange clouds upon the western sky,
The tranquil heaven's cloak in azure dye.
The day is dying to the darkening dusk,
Transition as suave as a pachyderm's tusk.
  Each morning breeze must slowly fade away,
  To steamy nights surrender must the day.

But before the darkness drop her jet black skirt,
At noon we'll celebrate my brainchild's birth.
We'll grill and eat and drink and dance as long
As you keep dancing to recitals of my song.
  Consume the fruits of cornucopia horn,
  I'll sleep in triumph that my child is born.

  Each morning breeze must slowly fade away,
  To steamy nights surrender must the day.

For Mama

It happened four slow summers long ago,
When Mama left for somewhere no one knows.
She reared me up 'though I didn't come from her,
And no one else as mother I'd prefer.
I cried on learning she've already died,
I'm now an orphan with no elder guide.
I bought two pails of biscuits for the wake,
It seemed improper to buy and bring a cake.
I rode on a trike to Balibago station,
The driver is of no relation.
I Balibago, vans bound to Lucena City,
Awaits me, filled with sadness, grief and pity.
I'll ride to my stepmom's funeral,
Among my fellow public general.
The sky was dark as if there'll be a heavy rain,
To rinse my self from misery and pain—
Dead is the last link to my childhood chain.
While on the tricycle I mutely wept,
  On both restraining hands the pails I firmly kept,

And on my teary eyes you'll see I haven't slept.

That fifteen-minute ride seemed like eternity,
As if with nature there was no conformity.
The driver dropped me to the terminal of vans,
I stepped out deftly like some voiceless swans,
Pulled a ten-peso coin, (that's twenty cents to you),
And tried to pay the driver, in full view.
But he refused my mile and quarter fare,
I did not force him, 'though it isn't fair.
The van was waiting to be filled with people,
I think they feel not that there's a sad ripple.
My final sixty-mile journey starts here,
Two hundred pesos (dollars shy of four) to there.
By then, I thought, the ride is free to those who weep,
So cry I tried 'til I was lulled to sleep.
  With eyes already dry, I did not shed a tear,
  And so I have to pay the fare in full, I fear.

Nouveau Riche

Thank God, at last! the hardships are *all over* (!),
Those pains now shrouded in oblivion's cover.
Those ceaseless, restless days and sleepless nights,
Eternal queues that end in ration fights.
Uncertainties of future mate(s) and heirs,
Afraid to even try to climb the stairs.
  But now these days I hear the plucking of the lyres,
  Way better than the noise of blowing tires.

A worry-free respite, a lighter shoulder,
I need no longer roll a massive boulder.
Of meats, and sweets, and seafoods on the table,
I get to eat all these more than I'm able.
It was not easy getting here,
I've brutalized my hungry body, Dear.
  And now I wear expensive coats and ties,
  And bloated with much trifled fruits and pies.

Froilan's, Ltd.

With thinning hair, a wide and shiny head,
I sleep on warmest, softest downy bed.
All Europe's finest spirits, and the sweetest wines,
I eat my steak where the president dines.
My bones are broken but my belly's full,
I'm denser than the fattest bull.
  So this is life, these pleasures I attain,
    I walk with the most expensive walking cane.

Froilan "Puroy" Manalo

The Nostalgic Prophet

Another century, another year,
My innocent years, those decades dear,
Just simply gone, the simple childish fun,
The Sunday ice cream cone, the bliss that age undone.
The fourteen-inch television set,
Plain black and white is all we'll get.
The ubiquitous Beetle to the movie house,
We laugh at comics with that iconic mouse.
We watch John Wayne quickly draw and shoot,
And marvel at how Kirk look snappy in his boots.
We watch those Mexicans that speak Tagalog,
Their pretty heroines came out of the fog.
The day will come that Filipina ladies
Will speak Korean— among other maladies.
  The end is coming soon, the signs are here,
  We'll dine on the moon before the coming fear.

I hope these coming decades bring us back
The unadulterated life today we lack.

Froilan's, Ltd.

Beware the Trojan horse, but I the Commie present,
We'll eat with chopsticks, so be more prescient.
But better yet I'll sit and sip my coffee,
And use a silver fork to eat my toffee.
  Fresh from my desk straight to the printing press,
  My words shall cause us wearing eighties dress.

The Promise

Outdo my previous best, how hard it was,
I wore my reddest crest, yet ended lower class.
Unsatisfied was I to fill the supplement,
I won't cut edges for a compliment.
If this is not my life-long very best,
Then lay me rest with the showers in the west.
  But think of all the chapters that we've been through,
  The pure and filthy truths and rumors seen as true.

The best is yet to come, the second book,
For now my was and is, just simply take a look;
And then you'll see, the seed will sprout a tree,
Have patience, Rome wasn't built a day for free.
  I've laid foundations for the future publication,
  And we'll get paid the world's imagination.

About the Author

Froilan "Puróy" Manalo, is a part time writer, whose main occupation is as a factory worker.

He studied B. S. Secondary Education in M.S. Enverga University in his mother's hometown, Catanauan, Quezon, Philippines.

Puróy is now in his early forties, a bachelor who lives with only his pet kitten for company.

He currently resides in Candelaria, Quezon,

Philippines.

www.ingramcontent.com/pod-product-compliance
Lightning Source LLC
LaVergne TN
LVHW041628070526
838199LV00052B/3278